I AM READING

Albert's Raccoon

KAREN WALLACE

ILLUSTRATED BY
GRAHAM PERCY

BOSTON

For Henry—K. W.
For Gabriel—G. P.

KINGFISHER
a Houghton Mifflin Company imprint
222 Berkeley Street
Boston, Massachusetts 02116
www.houghtonmifflinbooks.com

First published by Kingfisher in 2001
This edition published in 2004
2 4 6 8 10 9 7 5 3 1
1TR/0604/AJT/GRS(GRS)/115SMA

LIBRARY OF CONGRESS CATALOGING-IN-PUBLICATION DATA
Wallace, Karen.
Albert's raccoon/Karen Wallace; illustrated by Graham Percy.
p. cm.—(I am reading)
Summary: Albert loves the raccoon that his uncle sends him, but the
mischievous creature causes an uproar when Albert takes him to his father's
candy factory.
[1. Raccoons—Fiction. 2. Candy—Fiction.] I. Percy, Graham, ill.
II.Title. III. Series.
PZ7.W1568Al 2004 [E]—dc22
2004007551

ISBN 0-7534-5717-2

Printed in India

Contents

Chapter One

One day Albert came home from
school and saw a large wooden
box sitting on the doorstep.
It was from his Uncle Fred.
"Oh dear," said Albert's mother.
"The last time Uncle Fred came
to stay he left two snakes under
his bed and a giant bat hanging
on the back of the bedroom door."

Her face turned
white just thinking
about it.

Albert's father rolled his eyes.
"And the time before that he
left a hippopotamus in the pond."

They all looked at the box again.

There was a letter pinned to

its side.

Dear Albert,
Please look after Rocky.
He eats frogs, chicken legs,
crabs, clams, apples, nuts,
beetles, and lizards.
I have gone to help a bear
with a sore head.
         Love, Uncle Fred

Albert opened the box.

A small black-and-white animal

with a striped tail climbed out.

It looked like a furry burglar.

It was a raccoon.

"Wow!" cried Albert.

"Oh dear," said his mother.

"Oh no," said his father.

"Churr-churr," said Rocky the raccoon.

For the rest of the day Albert and
Rocky played together.

They hunted for apples.

They cracked nuts.

They looked everywhere for lizards.

Soon they were the best of friends.

9

That night Rocky slept
curled up in a box
in the kitchen.

That night Albert was
so excited he could hardly sleep.

He was excited because he was going

to visit his father's candy factory the

next day.

But most of all he was excited because

he had a brand-new, wonderful pet!

Chapter Two

Early the next morning a terrible
scream came from the kitchen.
Albert jumped out of bed
and ran down the stairs.
Albert's mother was standing
in the middle of the kitchen.
It looked like something out
of a strange dream.

The toaster was making spaghetti.

The pasta machine was making toast.

The fruit juice maker was peeling
potatoes.
And the washing machine was
cooking scrambled eggs for breakfast.

Albert's father walked into the
kitchen. Rocky opened one eye . . .
then quickly pretended to be asleep.
Albert's father looked at
Albert's mother.
Albert's mother looked at Albert.
Then everyone looked at
Albert's raccoon.

Rocky kept his eyes shut tight.

But everyone knew that raccoons

love fiddling with things.

And everyone could see the parts of

the washing machine that he was

trying to hide under his tail . . .

"That raccoon is not staying in my house!" cried Albert's mother.

"What are we going to do?" said Albert's father.

"I'll call the Raccoon Protection Society. They can pick him up today," said Albert's mother.

"Churr-churr!" said Rocky.

"I don't want Rocky to go!"
cried Albert.

"Don't worry, dear," said his mother.

"We'll get you another pet. A puppy
or a kitten maybe."

But Albert wasn't listening.

He was making a plan.

Chapter Three

Behind the kitchen door was Albert's old panda bear backpack.

It didn't look much like a raccoon, but his plan might just work.

Albert picked up Rocky and put him inside his shiny *new* backpack.

"Don't make a noise," whispered Albert. Rocky's bright eyes glittered. It was as if he understood every word.

Then Albert put the old panda bear backpack into Rocky's box and curled it up to look like it was asleep. Albert couldn't help grinning to himself. The Raccoon Protection Society would get a big surprise when they arrived to pick up Rocky!

19

Ten minutes later
Albert and his father set off for the
candy factory.
"Today is a very important day
at the factory, Albert," said his father.
"Why?" asked Albert.
"Mr. Caramel Chew is coming, so
nothing can go wrong."

Albert felt his face turn red.

"Who's Mr. Caramel Chew?"

he asked.

"Mr. Caramel Chew owns candy

stores all over the world," explained

Albert's father. "If he likes my candy,

he'll buy boxes and boxes of it."

"Churr-churr," said Rocky from

inside Albert's backpack.

"Excuse me?" said Albert's father.

Albert turned even redder.

"Er, er . . . I'm sure Mr. Chew will love your candy," he said quickly.

At that moment they drove through the factory gates.

Chapter Four

The telephone was ringing when
Albert and his father walked into
the candy factory.

"I won't be a minute," said Albert's
father. "Don't touch anything!"
Albert grinned. The factory was his
favorite place in the whole world.
It was full of machines that whistled
and rumbled and rattled.

At one end of the factory six huge beaters twirled around and around in six tubs full of a sticky candy mixture.

At the other end of the factory the candy mixture was baked in a giant oven.

Then it was cut into all kinds of shapes
and sizes by a special chopping machine.

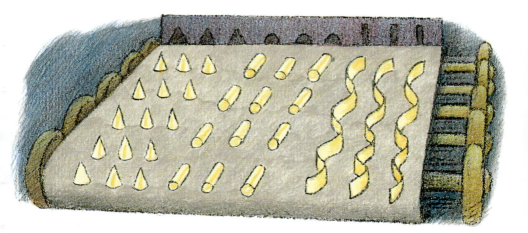

Finally all the candies were covered
with different colored coatings.

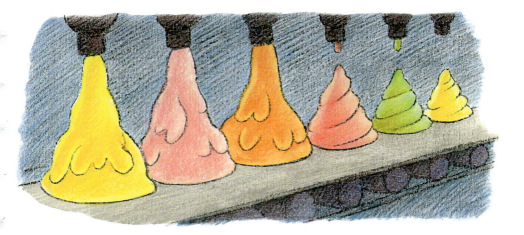

Bong!

Splatter!

The candies poured out of a huge silver tube onto an enormous tasting tray. That was Albert's favorite part.

Albert lifted his backpack off his shoulders.

"I'll show you around if you promise not to touch anything," he whispered to Rocky.

But when he opened the backpack, his stomach turned to ice.

Rocky had disappeared!

Chapter Five

BANG!

"Albert!" cried his father.

He ran from his office through a
snowstorm of marshmallows.

He ducked as thousands of gummy
babies shot through the air.

"I asked you not to touch—"

But he never finished his sentence.

Through the control room
window he saw a black-and-white
furry animal sitting in front of a
panel of levers and lights.

It was Rocky the raccoon—
and he was having the best
time ever!

Suddenly the machines went
crazy and made a noise they
had never made before.

Albert gulped.

Albert's father's eyes turned as big
as saucers.

Just then the factory door
swung open . . .

"Good morning!" said a deep, smooth voice.

A man wearing a brown-and-white suit and carrying a gold-topped cane walked in through the factory door.

"Mr. Caramel Chew, at your service," he said.

Albert's father's face turned the color of powdered sugar.

"Aren't you expecting me?" said Mr. Caramel Chew in a puzzled voice.

Albert's father opened his mouth, but no words came out.

Albert looked at Rocky.

Rocky looked back. His eyes twinkled.

Suddenly Albert knew everything would be all right. "Of course we're expecting you!" he said quickly. "And we have some wonderful candy to show you!"

"We do?" said Albert's father in a hollow voice.

"Of course we do," said Albert.

Mr. Caramel Chew looked from one person to the other.

He flipped open his notebook.

"Excellent!" he said. "Show me the way!"

Chapter Six

Albert, Albert's father, and

Mr. Caramel Chew stood in front

of the giant tasting tray.

It was empty.

"Never mind," said Mr. Caramel

Chew smoothly. "I'll come back

another day."

He snapped his notebook shut.

"Please wait!" cried Albert.

He gulped and looked up at Rocky in the control room. "I'm sure *something* will happen."

Albert's father rolled his eyes. Suddenly there was a whizz and a whirr and a clatter from the candy-making machine.

"Goodness me!" cried Mr. Caramel Chew. "Something *is* happening!"

WHOOOOOSH!

A waterfall of candy
poured out of the huge
silver tube and crashed
onto the tasting tray.
They were the
strangest-looking candies
you could ever imagine.
There were no gobstoppers
or gumdrops.
There were no jelly beans
or lollipops.
There was no bubble gum or
taffy or licorice.

Instead there were
sugary green frogs and
chewy chicken legs.
There were frosted pink
crabs and smooth
chocolate clams.
There were peppermint
lizards and crunchy
orange beetles.

They were just the kind of candies
a raccoon might like to eat!
Albert gasped and turned bright red.
What would Mr. Caramel
Chew say?

"Fantastic!" said Mr. Caramel Chew.
He clapped his hands and danced
around his cane.
"Your candies are absolutely
FANTASTIC!" he cried.
"I've never seen anything
like them!"
Mr. Caramel Chew grabbed
Albert's father by the hand.
"Congratulations, my dear sir!
I'll buy everything you have—and I'll
order one million more!"
"One million?" croaked Albert's father.
Mr. Caramel Chew threw back his
head and laughed.
"All right! TWO million!" he said.

At that moment Rocky the raccoon
scampered across the floor
and jumped into Albert's arms.

"Goodness gracious!" cried
Mr. Caramel Chew. He peered into
Rocky's clever eyes.

"Why, it looks like a raccoon!"
Albert's father patted Albert's
shoulders and tickled Rocky's ears.
"This isn't a raccoon," he said
proudly. "This is a small, furry,
candy-making genius."

He laughed and ruffled Albert's hair.
"And he belongs to my son, Albert!"
Albert looked up.
"Does that mean I can keep him
forever?" he whispered.
"Forever," said Albert's father
with a smile.

About the author and illustrator

Karen Wallace is an award-winning writer and has published more than 70 books for children. She was born in Canada, where she lived with her family in a log cabin. "We had friends with a pet raccoon. It lived in their house," says Karen. "The only problem was that the raccoon took everything apart at night—so they had to build him a little home in the garden. That was the raccoon I was thinking about when I wrote this story."

Graham Percy was born and raised in New Zealand. He came to London, England, to study at the Royal College of Art and has illustrated many books for children. Graham has never met a real raccoon, but he says, "Sometimes my studio looks as if Rocky has been in there, playing with my paints and knocking pencils all over my desk!"

Strategies for Independent Readers

Predict
Think about the cover, illustrations, and the title
of the book. What do you think this book will be about?
While you are reading think about what may
happen next and why.

Monitor
As you read ask yourself if what you're
reading makes sense. If it doesn't, reread, look
at the illustrations, or read ahead.

Question
Ask yourself questions about important ideas
in the story such as what the characters might
do or what you might learn.

Phonics
If there is a word that you do not know, look carefully
at the letters, sounds, and word parts that you do know.
Blend the sounds to read the word. Ask yourself if this is
a word you know. Does it make sense in the sentence?

Summarize
Think about the characters, the setting where the
story takes place, and the problem the characters faced
in the story. Tell the important ideas in the beginning,
middle, and end of the story.

Evaluate
Ask yourself questions like: Did you like the story?
Why or why not? How did the author make the story
come alive? How did the author make the story fun to
read? How well did you understand the story? Maybe
you can understand it better if you read it again!